Joey's Birthday Wish

Story by Matthew Lambert

Illustrations by Victoria Vebell Bruck

RSVP

RAINTREE
STECK-VAUGHN
PUBLISHERS
The Steck-Vaughn Company

Austin, Texas

1 2 3 4 5 6 7 8 9 0 RRD 99 98 97 96 95 94

Library of Congress Cataloging-in-Publication Data

Lambert, Matthew, 1981-
   Joey's birthday wish / story by Matthew Lambert; illustrations by Victoria Vebell Bruck.
      p.   cm. — (Publish-a-book)
   Summary: Joey gains a new appreciation of his home and belongings after he sees first-hand what life is like for the homeless.
   ISBN 0–8114–7273–6
   1. Children's writings, American.   [1. Homeless persons — Fiction.
2. Wishes — Fiction.   3. Birthdays — Fiction.   4. Children's writings.]
I. Bruck, Victoria, ill.   II. Title.   III. Series.
PZ7. L16965Jo 1995
[Fic] — dc20   94-40451
                                                                    CIP   AC

To my family for their love and support; to Mrs. Cindy Pharr for her dedication; and to homeless kids everywhere, that their wishes might come true. — M.L.

To my Joey, thank you for all your help, support, and love all these years. — V.V.B.

"If wishes were horses, beggars would ride," Mrs. Parker sighed, after Joey wished for the third time that morning for a new video game.

"What?" Joey asked.

"It's a quotation, Joey."

"What does it mean?" Joey asked again.

"Well, why don't you think about it awhile and see if you can figure it out."

"Okay, Mom," Joey called over his shoulder as he ran out the door. "I'm going to Whippoorwill Hill."

Whippoorwill Hill was Joey's favorite place in the whole world. He could see more than a mile in many directions. It was a good place to play and to think.

When he reached the top, Joey marveled at the blazing autumn scenery. The forest spread out below in a wild mosaic of crimson, saffron, and amber. As he gazed in awe at the view surrounding him, the ear-piercing shriek of a hawk caught his attention. Joey watched the red-tailed hawk gliding in the stiff breeze. Suddenly, the hawk swooped down to capture some unsuspecting prey.

"I wish I could soar like that hawk," thought Joey.
His mom's words echoed back to him. "If wishes were
horses, beggars would ride." What *did* that mean?

During supper, Mrs. Parker said, "Joey, I'm going into the city tomorrow to shop for your birthday dinner. Would you like to come along?"

"Sure, Mom," he replied eagerly. Joey loved going into the city — the sights and sounds of a busy place, airplanes overhead, traffic whizzing by, and people hurrying here and there. Joey wished he could live in the city. Once again, he recalled his mother's words, "If wishes were horses, beggars would ride."

The next morning dawned bright and clear and crisp. As Joey and his mom approached the city after their long drive, Joey's excitement began to build.

12

They passed tall buildings, busy shopping centers, and superhighways. Mrs. Parker drove carefully through the city traffic, finally turning into a huge shopping mall.

13

Joey knew that the first stop would be the big toy store. He couldn't wait to see all the toys. He knew that when he blew out the candles on his birthday cake, he would get to make a wish. For as long as he could remember, his birthday wishes had always come true. The brightly colored package that was saved for last was always what he had wished for.

As they entered the toy store, Joey's eyes sparkled. There were trucks and bulldozers, robots and cars, and much, much more. There were so many things he wanted to have. How would he ever make up his mind?

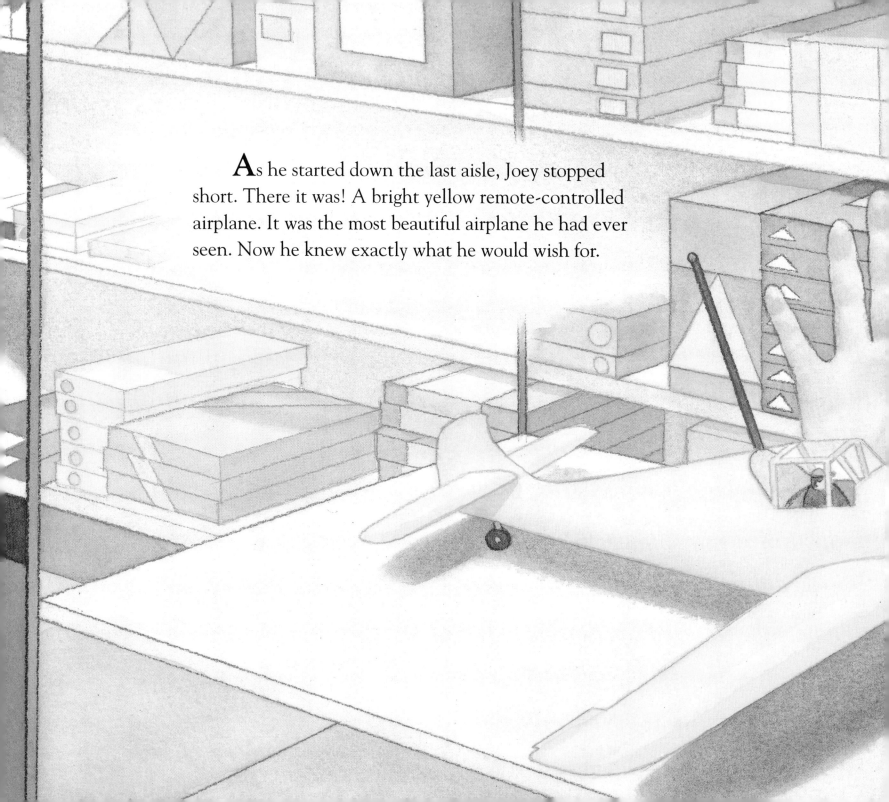

As he started down the last aisle, Joey stopped short. There it was! A bright yellow remote-controlled airplane. It was the most beautiful airplane he had ever seen. Now he knew exactly what he would wish for.

19

When they completed their shopping and began the journey home, Joey couldn't stop thinking about the yellow airplane.

"Oh no!" exclaimed Mrs. Parker. "We've taken a wrong turn."

Joey looked out of the window. The tall buildings were still there, but they looked different somehow. Instead of great shopping malls, small cluttered shops lined the streets.

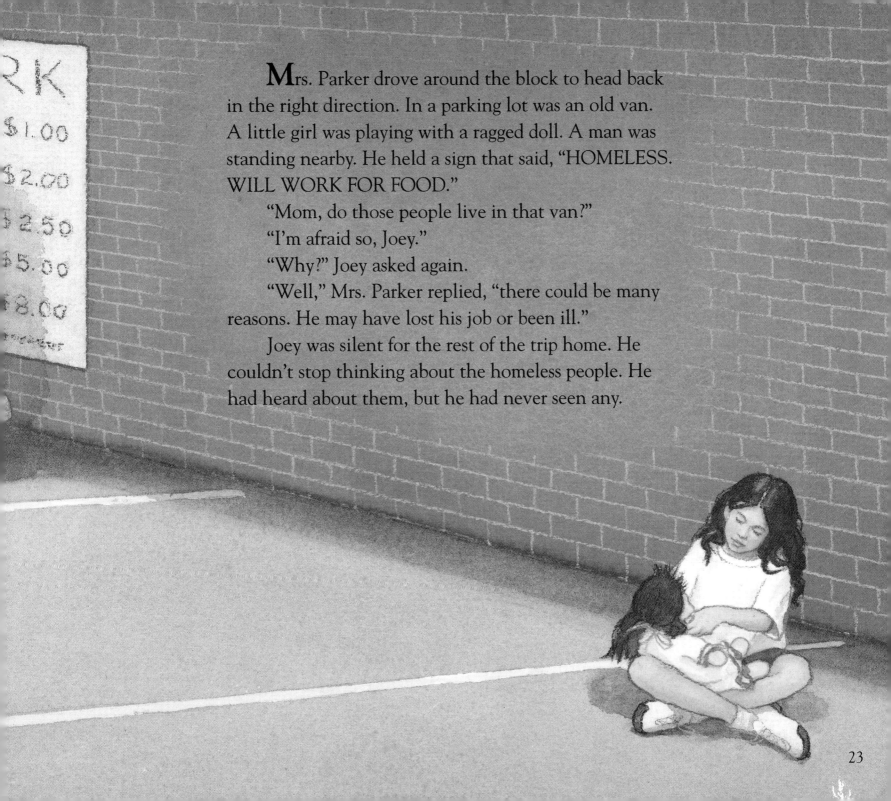

Mrs. Parker drove around the block to head back in the right direction. In a parking lot was an old van. A little girl was playing with a ragged doll. A man was standing nearby. He held a sign that said, "HOMELESS. WILL WORK FOR FOOD."

"Mom, do those people live in that van?"

"I'm afraid so, Joey."

"Why?" Joey asked again.

"Well," Mrs. Parker replied, "there could be many reasons. He may have lost his job or been ill."

Joey was silent for the rest of the trip home. He couldn't stop thinking about the homeless people. He had heard about them, but he had never seen any.

23

The day of his birthday, Joey was up early.
Mrs. Parker was busy in the kitchen getting ready
for the grandparents, aunts, uncles, and cousins who
would come later that day. Joey kept thinking about
his birthday wish. This time, he would cross his
fingers as he blew out the candles.

After the birthday dinner of all Joey's favorite
foods, the lights were dimmed. Mrs. Parker came out of
the kitchen with the birthday cake, candles flickering
brightly. Everyone sang "Happy Birthday."

27

Joey leaned over to blow out the candles. As he took a deep breath, he thought again of the homeless family he had seen. Suddenly, Joey knew the meaning of the quote, "If wishes were horses, beggars would ride." He thought of the wonderful dinner he had just eaten, the presents waiting to be opened, his cozy room and warm, soft bed. He had never been hungry and never been without a place to live in his whole life.

29

Then he remembered all of the wishes he had made in the last few days: a new video game, to fly, to live in the city, and especially the big yellow airplane. Joey knew he needed none of these things. How could he have been so selfish?

He realized that if all his wishes came true, soon nothing would have any meaning for him. There would be no reason to strive for anything. A wish should be saved for something really special.

Finally, Joey knew exactly what he would wish for. He closed his eyes tightly, crossed his fingers, and made his wish. He took a deep breath and blew out the candles. A slow smile crept across Joey's face. After all, his birthday wishes always came true.

Matthew Lambert, author of **Joey's Birthday Wish**, resides in Iuka, Mississippi, with his parents, Robert and Catherine, and an older brother, Taylor. Matthew is fond of animals and has lots of them, including a pet mule.

As a sixth-grade student in Iuka Middle School, Matthew was sponsored in the 1994 Publish-a-Book Contest by his teacher, Mrs. Cindy Pharr. Matthew's inspiration for his story grew out of a real-life experience he had when his family traveled to a nearby city to shop. Living in a small town, Matthew had never seen a homeless person and was deeply moved by the sight of one.

Matthew holds the distinction of being the only author to win the Publish-a-Book Contest twice. His previous story, *My First Spring*, won the 1993 Publish-a-Book Contest. Matthew was also chosen as the

recipient of the Alexander Fischbein Young Writer's Award once again. This award was established in memory of Alex Fischbein, a writer who died at the age of ten, to encourage young students to write and submit their works for publication.

Matthew's favorite subject is science, and he would like to become a veterinarian. He is an active member of the Tishomingo County Humane Society. His hobbies include reading, swimming, writing, taking care of his animals, and practicing the Japanese art of origami.

The twenty honorable-mention winners in the **1994 Raintree/Steck-Vaughn Publish-a-Book Contest** were Dennis J. Lee, Bowen School, Newton, Massachusetts; Jessica Stephen, Harborside School, Milford, Connecticut; Cassandra Gaddo, Southview Elementary School, Waconia, Minnesota; Emily Hinson, Robert E. Lee Elementary School, East Wenatchee, Washington; Jessie Manning, Rice Lake Elementary School, Maple Grove, Minnesota; Neil Finfrock, Brimfield Elementary, Kent, Ohio; Andrew Campbell, St. Eugene's School, Santa Rosa, California; Tiffany McDermott, St. Rose of Lima School, Freehold, New Jersey; Laura Dorval, Riverside Middle School, Chattaroy, Washington; Alison Taylor, Fisher Elementary School, Oklahoma City, Oklahoma; Kendra Hennig, East Farms School, Farmington, Connecticut; Lisa Walters, Northeast Elementary School, Kearney, Nebraska; Hunter Stitik, Forest Oak Elementary School, Newark, Delaware; Jamie Pucka, Rensselaer Central Middle School, Rensselaer, Indiana; April Wagner, Monte Vista Middle School, San Jacinto, California; Elizabeth Neale, Clifton Springs Elementary School, Clifton Springs, New York; Rachel Kuehn, Roseville Public Library, Roseville, California; Carolyn Blessing, John Diemer School, Overland Park, Kansas; Kelsey Condra, Grace Academy of Dallas, Dallas, Texas; Michael Gildener-Leapman, Charles E. Smith Jewish Day School, Rockville, Maryland.

Victoria Vebell Bruck has been an illustrator for twenty years. She grew up in Connecticut and lived in the area until she and her husband moved to Austin, Texas, three years ago. The majority of her artwork has been for book covers, but her illustrations have also appeared in magazines and in advertising. This is her first children's book.